'"I love how you love things," someone who loves her tells Jo Ann Beard. That love is one reason *Festival Days* is such a great book. Another is her flair for describing those things in vibrant and felicitous prose. Beard honours the beautiful, the sacred and the comic in life, and for life's inescapable cruelties and woes she offers the wisdom of a sage' Sigrid Nunez, author of *What Are You Going Through* and the National Book Award-winning *The Friend*

'Jo Ann Beard's work impresses me no end. Funny without being sitcomish, self-aware without being self-absorbed, scrupulous without being fussy, emotional without being sentimental, pointed without being cruel – I could go on and on with these distinctions, all in Beard's favour, but instead I'll just say that Jo Ann Beard is a fantastic writer, an Athena born fully formed out of her own painstaking head' Jeffrey Eugenides, author of *The Virgin Suicides*

'Beard's power comes from phrasings and insights that aren't just screaming for likes. Few writers are so wise and self-effacing and emotionally honest all in one breath ... she effects an intimacy that makes us want to sit on the rug and listen' Sara Lippmann, *Washington Post*

'[Beard's] books are worth the wait. A master of sensory details, she also writes with humour, melancholy and a love of animals that never borders on saccharine ... In her work, even everyday moments gleam with significance' Michele Filgate, *Los Angeles Times*

'A master of creative nonfiction, Beard explores life's most salient moments through facts that she sometimes fractures' Amy Sutherland, *Boston Globe*

'Intimate, intelligent, intense – and ultimately comforting ... Like a hot-water bottle for grief, these honest, beautiful essays and stories take on the death of a beloved animal, a friend's illness, getting dumped by a partner and other tragedies few escape' *People* (Book of the Week)

'Charged with fine detail ... Beard is so good at what she does ... In Beard's book, writing works like compound interest, each experience building on the last, which built on the one before' Ellen Akins, *Minneapolis Star Tribune*

'I can't think of a writer who puts words to our most difficult moments as adroitly as Beard – who so steadfastly refuses to cut away when things get tough' Dan Kois, *Slate*

'Beard's syntax is immortalising ... An acute quality in Beard's work makes the stories feel lived, even alive, as if they are still happening' Rachel DeWoskin, *Los Angeles Review of Books*

'Beard renders her own life and the lives of others with characteristic precision ... With each piece, she presses the essay form into new, more intimate territory'
*Poets & Writers Magazine*

'An absolute marvel ... as Beard demonstrates in her writing, life as we know it is full of bizarre, sad, beautiful, unbelievable, indescribable things – events that transform our real lives into surreal experiences' Chelsea Hodson, *BOMB Magazine*

'[Beard's] topics range from the quotidian to the fantastic, but all are anchored by observant, beautifully written prose that's sure to rank among the year's best' *Town & Country* (Must-Read Books of Winter 2021)

'Imaginative and precise ... These sharp essays cement Beard's reputation as a master of the form ... [she] can evoke many emotions in a single stroke' *Publishers Weekly* (starred review)

# CHERI

**ALSO BY JO ANN BEARD**

*The Boys of My Youth*
*In Zanesville*
*Festival Days*
*The Collected Works of Jo Ann Beard*

# CHERI

## JO ANN BEARD

First published in Great Britain in 2023 by Serpent's Tail,
an imprint of PROFILE BOOKS LTD
29 Cloth Fair
London
EC1A 7JQ
www.serpentstail.com

First published in USA as 'Undertaker, Please Drive Slow' in *Am I
Blue?* in *Tin House*, issue no. 12, summer 2002, and as 'Cheri' in 2021
in *Festival Days*, a collection of short stories by the author, by Little,
Brown and Company, a division of Hachette Book Group, New York,
USA

Typeset in Freight Text by MacGuru Ltd
Printed and bound in Great Britain by Clays Ltd, Elcograf S.p.A.

A CIP record for this book can be obtained from the British Library

ISBN: 978 1 80081 785 2
eISBN: 978 1 80081 787 6

For Cheri Tremble
1950–1997

# CHERI

They came slowly down the street, two boys on bicycles, riding side by side through the glare of a summer afternoon. She's on the curb, and the sun is so bright and hot it feels like her hair is on fire. If she glances down, she can just see the rubber toes of her sneakers and the skirt of her sundress, the color of root beer. The boys are playing tug-of-war, leaning away from each other, front wheels wobbling, each grasping one end of a long black snake. They have pale matching hair that stands up like the bristles of a brush, and their mouths are open in silent, gleeful shouts. The snake is dusty and limp, but as they sweep past she sees its eye, wide awake, and the sudden flat ribbon of tongue, scarlet against the boy's white wrist.

This is the way Cheri's life is passing in front of her eyes, in random unrelated glimpses, one or two a day. They come from nowhere, the bottom of her brain, and are suddenly projected, intense and silent as the Zapruder film, while she watches. This morning as she was eating her oatmeal what passed in front of her eyes was her first husband, shirtless against a blue sky, tying up tomato plants. And now tonight, climbing into bed, the Riley boys with a river snake, circa 1955.

The bed feels like a boat on choppy water. She pulls her foot out from under the covers and rests it on the floor for ballast. That's what they used to say to do if you were drunk and had the whirlies. The phone rings in the living room and she hears Sarah's voice against the sound of the television. In those old TV shows and movies way back when, the husband and wife had to keep one foot on the floor during the bed scenes. It meant everything was friendly instead of passionate. Well, the trick is working here tonight, the nausea is receding.

A wand of light appears and then widens; Bone's head is framed in the doorway. He pads across the room on velvet cat paws and freezes when he sees her bare foot on the floor. He stares at it in the dark with wide terrified eyes, then takes his place next to Nimbus at the foot of the bed. The girls were helping her burn leaves all afternoon and now the cats smell like marijuana smoke. In this morning's vision, her first husband was standing waist-deep in some unkempt garden of theirs, hair in a ponytail, a small frown on his face, and a joint behind his ear. Back in New York, one of her chemo doctors had discreetly mentioned marijuana for nausea, and some kind soul had given her a plate of pot brownies that she had taken like medicine, eating one each morning for breakfast. She had wandered her Brooklyn apartment in a state of muffled calm, straightening bedspreads and dish towels and staring slack-jawed out the window until the monster awoke, nudged her back into the bathroom, pushed her face in the toilet.

Cheri stretches her toes reflexively, making sure they still work. She's seen pictures of her spine, ghostly negatives resting against a light box, and the cancer looks tiny, like a baby's grasping fingers. The doctor used a pencil with bite marks on it to show her the metastases: Here, here, and a tiny bit here. Her relaxation is so complete that the bed now has the soothing, side-to-side rocking motion of a train car. Scenery floods past, mostly clumps of rocks and little hillocks scattered with dark green trees. *Here, here, and a tiny bit here.* A farm, a collie dog loping next to the tracks, and then the sudden startling face of a long-dead uncle. It seemed like he had shouted something but she couldn't catch it.

"What?" she says into the dark.

"Nothing," Sarah whispers from the doorway. "I was just standing here for a second."

How had she done it, raised these two exotic wild-haired daughters? They were back in Iowa City temporarily, crowding their personalities into her little house, blearily eating bowls of cereal each morning before raking the leaves into bright piles or spading the flower beds. The rest of the time they lounged on the front porch where they kept their packs of cigarettes, smoking and having long murmured squabbles, going from flannel shirts to tank tops and back to flannel shirts again as the fall afternoons waxed and waned. Every evening one of them would ease out of the house and clunk away in motorcycle boots and vivid lipstick, down the street and into the neighborhood tavern. They mostly took turns, one of them swigging beers, shooting pool, and punching up embarrassing, elderly jukebox songs, the other at home sprawled in front of the television, pale as a widow, drinking cups of fragrant tea and eating malted milk balls by the handful.

Tonight it's Sarah standing silent against the door frame, staring intently at the floor, hands gripping elbows, listening to her mother breathe. Cheri feels the stirrings of a cough deep inside her lungs. It's the monster locked in the basement, and eventually it will storm up the stairs and burst forth, attacking her in her own home, swinging a mallet at her chest over and over. Once she can breathe again, she makes a joke out of it: I'm Buddy Hackett, I'm Gene Hackman.

Nobody even pretends to laugh at this anymore; they're too tired.

"I thought you were sleeping," Sarah says. "The phone was for you."

Cheri nudges a cat away from her hip, making room, and Sarah climbs in bed beside her. It's a slumber party minus the fun. She was awake; she could have taken the call.

"He said you should rest," Sarah answers.

Who said?

Besides *terminal* and *cancer*, there are no more final-sounding words in the English language than these. Jack Kevorkian. That's who.

And then, despite themselves, they are starstruck for a moment at the idea of this spry ghoul from the evening news picking up his phone in Michigan and dialing Cheri's little house in Iowa, with its polished floors and eccentric armchairs. Backlit from the hallway, the cats' ears are almost transparent, like parchment lampshades. They watch the humans in their giddiness, faces sharp and impassive.

They'll be wide-awake alive and I'll be dead, Cheri thinks suddenly. Not just the cats, but everyone. Sarah, Katy, her best friends, Linda and Wayne. Linda and Wayne's children, the lady at the pharmacy who calls her Churry instead of Cheri, the man covered in dirt and desperation who sometimes slept on her stoop back in Brooklyn. Her first husband, her second husband, *her own mother,* all those medical professionals.

His nickname is Dr. Death, and yet when it's over, he'll still be alive.

The lump was discovered during a routine mammogram two and a half years earlier. She spent the last normal afternoon of her life on the train, Baltimore to Penn Station, taking tickets and trying not to notice that an elderly passenger had a dog in her pocketbook. Amtrak had a rule against animals riding its trains, but unless someone complained, Cheri didn't intend to notice. She planned to frown at the lady when they got to Penn, but she didn't even do that since it was quitting time and she felt cheerful. The Chihuahua's tiny face was poked all the way out of the bag by then, smugly gazing about.

Before her appointment, she went to the gym, ran and sweated, saunaed, showered, and tried to fluff her hair up a little. She needed a haircut more than a mammogram, but what she really needed more than either was to find her Mastercard, which had better be home on her dresser, because otherwise she had no idea where it was. She walked to the radiology place in her running shoes, going over the past three days, mentally taking her credit card out at various moments—grocery store, dinner at Ollie's, a weak moment with an L. L. Bean catalog—and putting it back in her wallet. The waiting room was disappointingly full and so she looked at fashion models in a magazine and watched the other patients until she was called.

The X-ray technician was a young woman with cat's-eye glasses and an unprofessional sense of humor. She wore bright yellow clogs. Here comes the S and

M part, she said as the machine closed its jaws. Click, flash; other side. She collected the trays and went off to show the films to the doctor. Be right back, she said as she left the room. And didn't return.

Cheri sat waiting, searching her mind until she thought she might have located the credit card in the back pocket of her black jeans, which were probably stuffed in the hamper. As the minutes wore on and then on, her hearing became heightened and her hands turned damp and cold. She rubbed them on her paper shirt. There was activity up and down the hall, doors opening and closing, voices leaking out. After twenty-six minutes had passed, she no longer wanted the technician to return. Every time she heard footsteps in the hall she willed them in the other direction. *Get lost, get lost,* she said under her breath, and they did get lost, until once they didn't and then the knob turned and the room was filled with the starched air of courteous detachment:

"Doctor wants more films."

And that's how everything changed, not with the pronouncement, even, but with a woman's disengaged expression. The room was engulfed in a tinny silence as she worked, arranging Cheri like a mannequin, folding her against the stainless steel, placing an arm up here, a breast in there, sending her home. Once, a long time later, when Cheri's life was passing in front of her eyes, she caught a glimpse of it again—saw the bright yellow cartoon feet of the technician and then saw her own naked left arm, in slow, muted motion, rising obediently to embrace the machine.

The lump was a dreamy smear on the X-ray, barely there, unfeelable except in her throat when she tried to talk. She spoke to Linda late at night, each of them standing in a dark kitchen, one in Brooklyn and one in Iowa City. Lump, lumpectomy, chemo, Cheri said. Yes, Linda said, that's what they do. A silence in which both of them wished they were seven-year-old hellions again instead of what they were—a train conductor and a nurse; mothers; women who wore uniforms and looked sexy in them. Best friends since age five. It seems to be happening to both of them, although it isn't. For the duration of the phone call, they manage to remain calm.

And the illness proceeds on its trajectory, a knife, a scar, a plant-filled atrium where people sit in cubicles getting their treatments. One of the things she learns is how to vomit into a curved plastic trough while lying flat on her back. After six months another pale lump is photographed, no bigger but resolute, like a schoolyard bully who comes back even after getting a terrible pummeling. Linda waits for the phone call and when it comes she sits down. Lump, mastectomy, more chemo, Cheri says. Okay, Linda says, and she covers her face with one hand.

This time there's a tray of knives; she sees them right before the anesthesia erases her. When she awakens, her breast is gone, melted into a long weeping wound across her chest. The first time she sees it, she feels a strange numbness, a smooth blank where her shock should be. A day later the mortification is so profound and clamorous that she has to disconnect, like hanging up the receiver when someone is shouting into your ear. Her daughters fold gauze and tear tape and change her bandages without flinching. They seem larger to her in her new whittled-down state, like giantesses come to bathe and swaddle her. *I'm okay*, she says forty times a day, until she comes to believe it, and then they relax. Katy returns to school and Sarah finds a job down the street at a Starbucks instead of going back like she planned. They decided it between themselves, keeping Cheri in the dark, under the looming purple shadow of follow-up chemo.

It comes at her with talons and beak—after the first treatment, she winds up in the emergency room, tethered to an IV in a curtained cubicle, listening to the audio of what sounds like a television drama but isn't. An elderly woman calling out for help, a doctor speaking loudly and testily to an

Jo Ann Beard

underling, a man relentlessly berating his wife in Spanish while a baby cries at regular intervals, like a chorus. At six a.m. she and Sarah crawl back into a cab and ride home with their eyes closed as the sun comes up.

And it gets progressively worse, the exhaustion and illness so wretched that she feels like a dying animal. There is something of the barnyard about all of it—the earthiness, the smells, the sheer bovine physicality of being in such a body, plodding from the bed to the bathroom on tottering legs. During a particularly bad afternoon when Sarah is at work, she hears herself as if from a great distance. The sound she's making is resonant and sustained, like the lowing of a frightened steer.

And then gradually she's well, the monster scoured clean with a wire brush, slinking off to watch her from a distance. She doesn't care. Fuck the monster. She takes up running again and sits in the sauna breathing steam into her cells, a towel discreetly knotted over the hollow spot on her chest. Eventually the stares get to her and she decides to undergo reconstructive surgery. This is routine, a process by which tissue from the groin is fashioned into a breast, like building Eve from Adam. Only it isn't God running the construction crew, it's Sloan Kettering.

Something goes wrong on the operating table. She comes out of surgery shaped like a woman again but unable to walk, one leg slack and rubbery, refusing to hold her weight. Eventually she leaves the hospital on crutches and calls Linda from a chair in the center of her living room, staring into the kitchen at her cup of tea on the counter. They're going to waive my bill, she tells her friend. Nerve damage, Linda replies. Positioned wrong on the operating table, probably. Get them to help you.

But they remain thin-lipped and silent, unwilling even to diagnose the problem, let alone treat it. She tries everything from the crutches to a walker to a leg brace, hobbling, learning to carry her tea without spilling it but never figuring out how to work on the train without standing or walking. Disability runs out and Amtrak lets her go. She loses not only her paycheck but her pension and her benefits. She drags her leg up and down the street each day like a zombie with a crutch nestled against her new breast, while pedestrians eddy around her and joggers sweat in the July heat.

It's night of the living leg, she tells Linda.

Come home, Linda says.

So her friends visit her in pairs, bearing bubble wrap and boxes and small, meaningful gifts that have to be packed along with dishes and books. Nobody can believe this is happening, although they felt the same way about the lump, the chemo, the mastectomy, the other chemo. But crippled isn't cancer, and for that they're all grateful. They've heard that Iowa is beautiful. One of her former coworkers, a man from the Bronx, asks if she will have neighbors out there. She visits the clinic one last time, stumping past the waiting room filled with women in various states of deconstruction. The medical staff seem very pleased with how the breast turned out and mildly surprised that she's leaving but they know that cancer changes people, turns them around in significant ways.

*I can't walk,* she says tersely. I lost my job and my pension.

And Iowa truly is beautiful in September when she arrives. She moves into Linda and Wayne's spare room and sets to work getting back on her feet, literally. She undergoes physical therapy for numbness and foot drop, and the local doctors install something called a transcutaneous nerve stimulator, which works, slowly and miraculously.

She feels bionic and hopeful in her leg brace and dungarees, restored to her former Iowa self, sitting on the dark porch at night with Linda and Wayne and one or two of their children, cats wafting around their ankles while they talk and talk. During the days, she works on her leg, walking and stretching and balancing herself, practicing with the cane until she's almost like a regular person. They rake leaves right before a windstorm and wake the next morning to find them evenly distributed over the lawn again. They have barbecues and card games. She and Linda house-hunt with fervor, horrified at what they see until one day a little house on Davenport Street goes on the market and they get wild with excitement. Wayne looks it over and they scheme; Cheri calls her mother and arranges a loan, then lands a job in an optometrist's office where she doesn't have to stand or walk and can sit all day on a stool, her cane against the wall behind her. Within three months of arriving in Iowa, she has a house, a job, and a life.

This is her town now, bathed in pale January light, populated with students and bright, vivid women, the occasional interesting man. She hangs a string of white lights around her kitchen window and buys a tall, leafy schefflera tree for the living room that she replants in an orange-glazed pot. She talks on the phone and watches television in the evenings, drunk on coziness and midwestern domesticity. At some point she begins to sweat during the nights, waking up to a damp nightgown and clammy sheets. It develops into an Iowa head cold; she can barely breathe but it's nothing to her, a sniffle with a headache. Herbal tinctures from the health-food store, fruits, vegetables, good heavy bread, lots of soup. The cold recedes eventually and she's left with chapped nostrils and a large lump on the right side of her neck.

Fear moves into the little house with her, taking up residence in the back of her closet along with the down comforter that she can no longer use. The night sweats get worse, forcing her up and into the living room, where she knits to keep from touching the lump. She can't tell if it's sore or if she's just prodding it too much. It's definitely big. Linda is worried, although she's also reasonable; it could be a residual effect from the cold.

The doctor is circumspect, steepling her hands and furrowing her brow. Aspiration is called for, a long needle into the neck like something out of a Boris Karloff movie. She's the bride of Frankenstein, she's the girl in the thin nightie cowering as the monster peers through her window. Mostly she's Katy and Sarah's mother, and they rally again, Katy on the telephone, talking of boys and clothes, her voice alive with fear, and then Sarah, who's been living in the general vicinity, on her doorstep.

She walks with Sarah in Hickory Hill Park after the procedure is done. The trees are denuded still and the sky is like milk; their faces are raked by the damp wind but there's nowhere else to go and so they walk and think, not speaking. It's two years exactly since this all began. On the way back to the house, they hold hands like schoolchildren. Before the kettle can boil, the telephone rings; the doctor wants to see Cheri in her office.

Cancer in the lymph system, metastasized from the breast. Statistically speaking, two years at the outside, with aggressive treatment. Without it, much less.

They are sitting in upholstered armchairs in front of the doctor's desk, like applicants denied a bank loan. Sarah leans forward from the waist and sobs uncontrollably, her face on her knees, hands clutching her ankles. This is how she cried as a toddler when it was bedtime and the party was still going on. *This is my daughter,* Cheri thinks. *My other daughter is Kate.*

The doctor hands a tissue across the desk and watches Cheri intently. When finally she looks away, Cheri turns to Sarah and touches her arm. Sarah sits up, takes the tissue, and presses it into her face.

Don't cry, it's okay, Cheri hears herself saying. I had to go sometime.

The doctor doesn't disagree, which seems heartless, but also doesn't hurry them along, which seems kind. They collect referrals and then make their way through the waiting room and to the door, Sarah crying still, gently leading her mother. When they step outside into the dull afternoon light, Cheri is overcome with a feeling of weightlessness and vertigo. She's Fay Wray nestled in the monster's palm as he scales the skyscraper.

*

Fifth-grade skating party at Ames Pond. She can see Billy Mayfield's bare hand holding her mittened one as he pulls her along, her own feet in their pompommed ice skates scissoring beneath her as she keeps up. Crack the whip with a line of sweaty kids, and Cheri's at the end of it. Scenery whirls past—trash barrels, sparse evergreens, snow hut with faces grouped around a heater, the striped tail of her own stocking cap—and then the whip cracks and she's flung, hurtling across the ice on her back, turning once in slow motion as the clouds revolve, and then a sickening crunch. Through the ice and under, she plunges down in the dark water, skates sticking in the muddy bottom for an instant, and then rises slowly, spinning, until her head bumps on the underside of the ice. For one long surreal moment, before an arm reaches in, grasps the hood of her coat, and hauls her out, she is suspended under the warped ceiling of ice. Inside the roaring silence of the water, she looks up and sees the skates of the excited children congregating above her.

The flashbacks have begun now, coming to her when she's distracted in her kitchen, washing cups or staring into the fridge. Yesterday she was placing a flower in a vase—a lone iris, the color of grape soda—and suddenly saw a row of people yelling and shaking their fists at her. It bothers her for hours, until she finally figures out it was from back in her cheerleading days. The Ames Pond memory had been suppressed for thirty-six years until tonight. It rose unbidden, like a genie, as she eased the cork from a bottle of wine. What she had chosen to remember all these years was actually an addendum to the memory: Billy Mayfield returning her blue mitten the next day at school, the one she was wearing when she'd rocketed out of his grasp. He'd handed it to her in a brown paper lunch sack with Cheri's name written on it in blue ballpoint, a mother's spidery script.

They're drinking wine, waiting for Wayne to show up so they can get some dinner.

It's cold but they put on jackets and head to the patio. Another volunteer iris, this one a strange pale yellow, grows near the garage. Cheri's garden is a tangle still but she's sorting it out; the air is fragrant with compost and lilacs.

Aggressive treatment at this stage would mean a bone-marrow transplant. One thug beating another thug, with her in the middle. She's not going to do it.

People get through this, Linda says. We'll help you.

Never again, Cheri tells her. I said so the last time.

The bridal wreath bushes along the back fence are buried under tiers of ruffles. Each blossom is a small bouquet. They were married in the 1970s, Linda to Wayne and Cheri to Dave. Hippie intellectuals with garlands in their hair, intense frivolity, et cetera. Floating in and out of each other's front doors, macramé projects, and funky baby showers that included the men. Linda had two girls, then, later, a boy. Cheri had first borne Sarah, dreamy and social, then baby Kate, with her black hair and shy grin.

In her spare time, Cheri immersed herself in the tenets of the Socialist Party— which they all sort of agree with in theory, if not in practice—and moved from political idealist to political activist. She spoke her mind more and more: *I believe an injury to one is an injury to all . . . the concept of class- lessness gets to the heart of the matter—why it's so important to try and live it, put it into action, fight for it if need be. Without that you accept less.* Should have been a warning, but they were all taken by surprise when she left them, absorbed into another life that had more meaning for her. First to Chicago and then to the South, where she worked in factories and mills putting her principles into practice, shaping her life like wet clay until it hardened, leaving her in New York City years later, punching tickets on a train and liking it. She was always the type to do her ruminating alone, in the privacy of her own head, and back then, when she'd made the decision to leave her marriage and

Iowa, she'd simply announced it and then set about getting it done, ears stubbornly turned off to pleas and reason. A few weeks later she had driven away with Katy in the back seat, wide-eyed and silent, while Sarah sobbed in her father's arms, reaching out toward the disappearing car.

*No chemo.* She said so before and she's sticking with it. Her face is resolute in the narrowing light, unfaltering. Linda has seen this look before; right behind all that beauty and grief are the steel girders of pragmatism.

Of course, she hadn't stuck with the decision to let Dave keep Sarah. Bereft without her daughter, Cheri eventually got her back, doing penance then and for years after. This won't work that way; the penalty for refusing chemo is mostly death.

They sit quietly, watching Wayne as he approaches up the back walk. One look at their faces and he knows what the decision is.

"Smells like shit," he remarks as he passes the freshly fertilized garden.

Now there are three of them drinking wine under the darkening sky, although one is already, imperceptibly, being erased from the tableau. They speak of restaurants and narrow it down to Indian or Chinese. Wayne can go either way, although he's up for spicy. Linda is thinking good, healthy vegetables and brown rice. She stands and collects wineglasses, tucks the bottle under her arm. As Linda starts to move toward the house, Cheri reaches out and touches her sleeve in a silent, sideways gesture of gratitude. In this withering light, they could all be twenty again, in worn jean jackets and sneakers, Wayne in his baseball cap.

An injury to one is an injury to all. She's made her decision, then, and they'll all live with it. Or, rather, two of them will.

One month later, another night sky, this time over Mexico. There are clouds adrift, and now the big yellow moon has a dent in its head. She doesn't care; it's all beautiful: the Aztec-tiled motel courtyard, palm trees in huge terra-cotta urns, their fronds rustling like corn. Katy is out walking in the night air with the daughter of another patient, and Cheri is reclining poolside, watching satellites blink overhead and sipping a concoction they gave her at the clinic. It tastes quite good, actually, if you don't think about it. Sort of like a piña colada boosted with iron shavings.

They can say what they will about alternative therapy, but it's doing as much for her as the chemo ever did and there's no throwing up involved. Mornings at the clinic are spent getting laetrile treatments, administered intravenously by smiling Mexican women who wear traditional nurse's caps and an assortment of ankle bracelets. Afternoons are given over to consultations with staff members, who take her history and offer advice on ways to coax the monster back into its cage. Lion tamers holding out spindly chairs.

She spends hours knitting in the waiting room, surrounded by the shining, hopeful faces of the truly desperate. Today a gaunt and yet somehow baggy-looking man in a slogan T-shirt—the words LOVE ME, LOVE MY HOG over a picture of a Harley-Davidson motorcycle—confided to Cheri that six months ago he weighed over three hundred pounds and was still hitting the booze.

"First my liver give out for a while," he said, hollow-eyed and shivering, "and then this cancer set in." His daughter, a plain Pentecostal-looking girl in a sundress and tennis shoes, reached over and pressed the back of her hand against his forehead.

"You're dropping again," she told him quietly and left to wander the halls of the clinic, coming back with a wheelchair and an orderly. The motorcycle man waved to Cheri ruefully as they loaded him up.

"She don't let me suffer if she can help it," he said, staring up at the girl.

Les, a man Cheri knew from a seminar on purgatives, leaned forward after they were gone. "He might as well drink his coffee from a cup," he said. "Because no enema in the world will cure *that*." He was small and hairless, an elderly melanomic golfer in powder-blue pants. His son roams the peripheries of the waiting rooms and corridors in a suit and tie, snapping his briefcase open and shut, holding flowcharts up to the light like X-rays, one-finger typing on a laptop.

"He has to work wherever he goes," his father told Cheri. She made a polite gesture of commiseration but he shook his head. "He has to, he's the top over there. Nobody above him, from what I can tell." He ran a hand purposefully over his head and then looked at his palm. Nothing there, clean as a whistle.

"Wow," Cheri told him, and after a respectful pause she turned back to her knitting. Stitch, drop-stitch, stitch, cast off. In the waiting room, hours recede like a glacier, leaving bottles and wrappers in their wake. She is strangely moved by all of it, the sick people and their companions, the clean antiseptic smell, the inspirational messages calligraphed and framed on every wall. The sheikh character who moves from treatment room to seminar with an entourage of mournful draped women. The elderly lady in a copper wig who sat down next to her in the body, mind, and spirit lecture, reached for Cheri's hand, and clasped it for an hour, both of them staring ahead intently, holding on to the speaker's words like the bar of a trapeze.

That seminar closed with a quotation: *Worship the Lord your God, and His blessing will be on your food and water. I will take away sickness from among you.* Not exactly *The Communist Manifesto*, but who is she to judge. Her friend listened intently and then extricated her hand, took out a small battered notebook, and wrote *Exodus 23:25* at the bottom of a to-do list.

"You don't look a bit sick," she said to Cheri. Her eyes were wide and stark and her teeth didn't fit right. Cheri looked down at her own feet, brown in their sandals, Katy's red nail polish giving each toe its own personality.

"I am, though," she replied.

"I have bust cancer," the woman told her, whispering.

Today they ran into each other in the

corridor and embraced spontaneously, Cheri taking care not to set the wig askew. The woman's husband stood quietly at a distance, staring over their shoulders, holding a straw purse.

This afternoon she came upon Les's son, the businessman, right here in the courtyard. Huddled on a stone ledge, half inside an overwrought bougainvillea bush, he wore a suit with the tie loosened sideways, his usually smooth hair adrift and spiky from him running his hands through it. A parody of a drunken man, only it wasn't alcohol, it was grief. Surrounded by giant blank-faced purple blossoms, he sobbed into a cell phone, eyes shut, mouth wrenched wide open in a child's grimace.

Now the courtyard is empty and dark, lit only by the muted lamps hidden amid the fronds and ferns. At the very center, the pool shimmers in its own light, like Aqua Velva. Cheri drops her robe and slides into the water, cool and bracing. She does a slow backstroke until it tires her, turns over, dives, and comes up with her hair slicked away from her face like a seal or a woman who knows she's beautiful.

Courtesy of her mother, it all is. All Cheri had to do was ask. Fifteen thousand dollars, just like that, for palm trees and exotic blooming flowers, the muggy Amazonian glade-like feel of this courtyard. All from her mother and her mother's husband, who wrote the check without flinching, buying her, if not an actual future, then the promise of a future. And the miracle is that she now feels healthy, her insides rinsed and wrung out, her exterior massaged and polished, the very blood in her veins carbonated. And it isn't better living through chemo; it's simple and organic. Fruit, coffee, oxygen, and words. *You are loved, we love you, you can live, others have lived.*

The water now feels warmer than the air, amniotic. A familiar sound drifts over the stone wall, subdued and infectious: Katy's laughter. They've returned from their walk, chatting just outside the gate, oblivious to the open shutters and the acoustic properties of the narrow street. Cheri lets herself drift backward until she's floating again, the sound of indistinct voices overcome by the water lapping against her ears. Eyes closed, she summons an image of Katy, with her wide grin and flat Brooklyn accent, hoop earrings, raucous hair; when she was in the room, you couldn't look anywhere else, nobody could. Then Sarah, she of the beautiful, deceptively serene face, hair knotted behind her head in a careless bun, choosing her words thoughtfully, then speaking them in the broad cadences of the Midwest. They're interesting, Cheri thinks. Compelling. She imagines the two of them huddled inside the rhododendron bush in her front yard, like Les's son in the arms of the bougainvillea, weeping.

The moon is high in the sky now, looking smaller and less certain. Tiny, long-legged lizards run along the sidewalks. In just a few days she'll be back home, tending her garden with its sturdy, quintessential-Iowa flowers—morning glories, zinnias, black-eyed Susans, and the tall lavender coneflowers, with their rusty hearts lifted up toward the sun, petals flung backward like arms. *You can live.* For one prolonged, irrational moment, hope circles the court-yard like a great winged heron, banking slowly over the pool and the lawn chairs, the dark foliage, and then wheeling out into the night. Gone.

*Others have lived.* She won't be one of them. She feels it in her bones, quite literally.

The summer that follows is long and lumi-nous. They canoe down the Wapsipinicon River, a rowdy cavalcade of humans and their coolers, and camp along the reedy banks, faces sunburned and firelit, marsh-mallows melting and blackening on sticks, the green nylon glow of flashlights inside tents. They climb into the car—Linda, Wayne, Cheri and a pan of brownies—and take a road trip, fourteen hours of stupefying knee-high corn and then the mind-blowing Rockies in all their vertical splendor. An outdoor music festival in Telluride—bands they've heard of and bands they've never heard of, old tie-dyed dudes in stretched-out T-shirts and slender gray ponytails, and the new generation of hippies with radiant, stoned faces, hair dreadlocked into felt. They forgo the brownies and hike a steep mountain trail, Cheri faltering only once, when Wayne tries to haul her up onto a boulder so she can see the vista. It's her mind, not her body—the vertigo of seeing it all fall away in front of her, leaving nothing but bright air and the strange shadows of clouds far below.

The new house turns out to be hotter than expected, and the snow peas don't take off the way she thought they would, but who can complain about sun-drenched rooms and vines that produce flowers instead of food? She drives out into the Amish countryside one afternoon, returning with a black bear cub of a puppy that she names Ursa. They take long surreal walks together through the cemetery down the street, the puppy dragging her leash among the tombstones and Cheri ambling behind, reading the inscriptions and doing the math. Forty-six years is a long time if you look at it a certain way. Ursa is her seventh dog.

The glimpses from her past are benign and interesting—the sullen face of a beautiful girl framed in a Dairy Queen window; the chrome-and-tan dashboard of an old Beetle, rearview mirror draped with Mardi Gras beads; a gnarled and mossy live oak standing in the middle of a chicken-scratched, red-dirt yard; and once, amazingly, what had to be her own tiny feet, grasped and lifted into the air in the classic pose of a diaper change. Weird. And she keeps them to herself, these unportentous images, as she does the gradual onset of pain. By September the cancer has divided itself like an emigrating clan, dispersing to her liver, lungs, and spine.

She takes the news stoically, nodding. It's fall and she could make it to spring, and they might be able to shrink the spinal tumor with radiation, enough to delay paralysis, keep her mobile for a while. They show her the films, and she stares transfixed at the perfect curve of her own spine caught and held by the shadowy fingers of the monster. *Here, here, and a tiny bit here.* The doctor sets his pencil down on the desk and she stares at it, composing herself, willing away the claustrophobic images of last summer, the botched surgery, her leg dragging behind her in the swirling Brooklyn heat, numb foot scraping along the sidewalk. A zombie, a reanimated corpse. All that for this.

It might not happen, the doctor tells her. Other things might happen first.

She takes that to mean death. In the context of paralysis, it seems comforting.

We can keep you comfortable, he says reassuringly. If it comes to that.

But I can't tolerate pain medication, she says. They never found anything that didn't make me vomit.

He writes something on her chart and closes it, holds out his hand.

And this, of course, is when the world turns glamorous. Her daughters look like movie stars in their low-slung pants and pale autumn complexions. The trees on her street vibrate in the afternoon sunlight, the dying leaves so brilliant that she somehow feels she's never seen any of this before—fall, and the way the landscape can levitate with color, and even her simple cup of green tea in the afternoons, with milk and honey in a thick white mug. Warm. Her hand curled around it, or the newspaper folded beside it, or a halved orange on a blue plate sitting next to it. It's all lovely beyond words, really.

Even the pain has a sharp, glittering realness to it, like a diamond lodged in her hip. She ignores it, gardening, pruning the dead foliage, sorting out the pumpkin vines, and still she walks each day, abandoning the stone cemetery for the dazzling woods at Hickory Hill. Troops of shiny-headed Cub Scouts move through the park, picking up gum wrappers and cigarette butts, stopping to pet Ursa, jostling each other, asking if she bites. They never heard of the name Ursa, but there's so much they haven't heard of that they take it in stride.

"Our dog got put to sleep from a brain tumor," a little boy tells Cheri. "His name was Pete and it might have been from eating grass with pesticide on it." He examines Ursa's head, lifting her ears and looking inside, then stands up. "This one seems okay," he says with an air of mild disappointment. He's smaller than the rest, compact and green-eyed, with a tumultuous stand of dark hair. An early version of all the men she's ever loved.

When he lopes away, Cheri feels strangely alone, but not unpleasantly so. Today the sky feels like company, and this winding orange-and-yellow trail. The diamond glints suddenly, causing her to gasp and squint her eyes. The pain sometimes is raucous, frightening; other times, it's a dull glow in her chest, like she's inhaling embers. It's her spine she can't stop thinking about, the recurring, disquieting image of being alive inside a dead body. Ursa turns toward home and Cheri follows at a distance, noticing how her knees bend and straighten with each step.

# Cheri

The girls are burning leaves next to the curb, great crackling piles of them. She sits on the front steps with her afternoon tea and watches, not speaking even when spoken to. She just wants to rest everything, her body, her mind. Unbidden, as she brings the white cup to her lips, a memory appears: Her refrigerator in an apartment down south, from the time when she worked in an airplane factory cleaning parts, up to her elbows in toxic gunk all day, despising it. A Suzuki quote, sent to her by a sympathetic friend, pinned to the scarred door of the fridge where she could see it each evening.

*When you do something, you should burn yourself up* completely, *like a good bonfire, leaving no trace of yourself.*

The girls pause to lean on their rakes, Sarah talking, Katy shaking out her hair, re-tying it. The fire has reduced itself to a thin meandering plume, like cigarette smoke, while leaves continue drifting down from the sky. *Burn yourself up completely.* That's it, then. She stands and looks at her daughters, raking coals in the waning light.

"I'm done," she tells them.

She doesn't think of it as killing herself; she thinks of it as killing the monster. That's why a gun would be so satisfying. But impossible, of course, given her circumstances. With window-leaping, you have a crowd, and in Iowa City that could mean one or two acquaintances. Drowning isn't possible; she tried it. In the bathtub, just as an experiment, to see if she'd have the nerve.

No one tells her not to do it. She isn't the kind of person you say that sort of thing to. Instead, everyone grows silent and wary, both daughters vacating the house for long hours, coming home for meals, steamed vegetables and instant rice or carryout from a downtown restaurant. Burritos dumped on a platter, refried beans shoveled into a bowl. Katy serving it up, Sarah pushing it around her plate. Cheri sipping ice water, lost in the pros and cons of her afternoon's research.

"Did you know a person of my weight

would have to fall fifteen feet to break her neck?" she asks suddenly. That's why people like to hang themselves in barns, where they can step off a rafter. Works better that way, otherwise you've got the problem of dangling there until suffocation occurs. No barns in the vicinity, unfortunately, but there is a garage. She's still going back and forth on asphyxiation.

Katy and Sarah stare at her, unblinking, forks suspended.

"No, I didn't," Sarah says finally.

So much for dinner. The girls clear the table without a word and adjourn to the living room and the evening news. Cheri stays in her spot, chewing ice cubes and waiting for Linda, who has taken to stopping by each evening. Pills would probably be the best, but whenever you hear *suicide attempt,* it's pills, and whenever you hear *suicide,* it's something more decisive—a bullet, a rope, a long sparkling plunge from a bridge.

The cough begins its slow ascent, giving her time to brace for it. Rattling and chaotic, it sounds like a paint can filled with gravel and rolled across the floor. By the time it's over—the gravel slowly diminishing to sand, shifting, allowing her to breathe again—Linda is beside her and the girls are in the doorway. Ursa moves from one to the next, offering a rawhide bone.

"You eat?" Linda asks, eyeing the dishes in the sink.

"I'm eating water," Cheri tells her, holding up the glass of ice.

In the living room, Vanna White prowls the row of letters in a dress as gauzy and form-fitting as a shroud. The television is always on now, one show melding into another, nobody really watching and nobody able to turn it off. As the evening progresses, they stare into the muted flickering light, first Sarah and Katy, then Sarah and Cheri, then just Sarah. At eleven o'clock the phone rings, a man asking for Cheri Tremble.

"She's in bed," Sarah tells him, "but she might still be awake."

"No, no," he says. "Let her rest if she can."

Cheri had written the letter outlining her situation, her intention, and asking for his help only a few days before. He plucked it out of his stack of appeals and responded immediately—the impending paralysis and her inability to tolerate painkillers were the deciding factors. If the medical records support her account of what's going on, Kevorkian is willing to help.

It's all true, Sarah whispers.

The living room is dim, lit only by the moonglow of the television. It all looks unfamiliar suddenly, and temporary, like a movie set. Kevorkian sounds just like a regular doctor, only sympathetic. He asks Sarah several questions—about Cheri's support system, how much care she needs, what her pain levels are like right now. Before hanging up, he explains that his patients have to come to him; he can't go to them.

He laughs at this, ruefully, and Sarah laughs too. She has no idea why.

In the dark bedroom at the end of the hall, Cheri is floating, unaware. The sleep train is just leaving the station, tracks unspooling like a grosgrain ribbon. The familiar Amtrak scenery rocks past: sparse woods, long brilliant flashes of water, the ass-end of a Delaware town, row houses with garbage bags taped over the windows. A neighbor from her childhood hangs sheets on a line wearing a housedress and men's shoes; as the sleeping car passes, the neighbor turns, watching its progress, shielding her eyes from the sun. A farm dog, running too close to the tracks, and then the face of someone she may have known once, an uncle, perhaps, gaunt and shadowed, telling her something she can't quite hear.

"What?" she says into the dark.

It's left up to her to set the date; Kevorkian is flexible. It's October now, and Cheri explains that she wants to make it through Christmas.

"Oh, I hope much longer," he says.

This touches her deeply for some reason, his empathetic response, his hope that she can remain alive as long as possible. He doesn't even know her! His voice is soothing over the telephone, and kind. More like a pastor than a doctor, really, but the medical questions he asks are sharply intelligent. For the first time Cheri is able to describe the pain in unminimizing terms. The relief of this causes tears to course down her cheeks, although her voice remains steady and businesslike.

She's to contact Neal, his assistant, when she has a date. Neal will give her directions on what to do then. For now, just try to be comfortable, get what she can out of her days, settle her affairs. And tell only the people who must know.

Kate, Sarah, Linda, Wayne.

She dresses as herself for Halloween— starkly thin, the extraneous flesh chiseled from her face, neck, wrists—and doles out chocolate bars to a sporadic procession of Disney characters and unraveling mummies. One boy with fangs and a plunging widow's peak hauls his sister up onto the porch, a tiny blonde in a Pocahontas outfit.

She holds her bag open distractedly, mask atop her head, peering past Cheri into the living room.

"The lady who lived here before died," she says. "And we've got her parakeet."

Her brother glances up at Cheri and then quickly away. "She's lying," he says apologetically, dragging the little girl off the porch and into the darkness. The dog follows them for a moment and then materializes again in the porch light, wagging her tail at the bowl of candy.

Ursa will go with Sarah, and the cats probably with Linda, unless Katy speaks up. This house to her mother, who paid for it. She spends the next week sorting through her belongings, musing, then composes a will and places it in the top drawer of her dresser. To the Petersons she writes:

Linda, please take my gardening hat, the one I wore at Telluride. Wayne, you could use a good corkscrew. I'm fond of my brass one, made in Italy (at least I think it's brass). I've had it about seventeen years. Brandice, help yourself to your favorite sweater, and Kailee, to your favorite piece of jewelry. Schuyler, take my fishing pole and catch some big ones for me, okay? TJ can have my assistant conductor hat pin from when I worked on the trains in New York City. It should be where this will is.

Her daughters, of course, are more difficult. The lists have to be weighed, items shifted back and forth until a precarious balance is achieved:

Sarah, I'd like for you to have my jade necklace, silver tea set, darkroom equipment, camping stuff, crystal vase, my books, and my exercise bike. Also the family heirloom silver and brass curios and the picture of McGregor and the blanket from Mexico.

Kate, I'd like for you to have my silver chain necklace, ruby ring (which Gramma has), camera and accessories, rocking chair, bike, round mirror, word processor, stereo and political books and pottery from Mexico.

By early November her yard is done. If there were going to be a next year, she would have moved some of the plantings— the peonies closer to the house, the little yew farther away. But it's set for now, everything mulched, her tools cleaned and stored in the basement. By the time she has her household in order, the exhaustion has become so acute it feels like sandbags are hanging from her limbs; sometimes just pushing the hair back from her face takes more energy than she can summon.

*The lady who lived here before died.* The body devolves into compost, but we live on in our parakeets. She dreams of them, fluorescent feathers glimpsed through dark foliage. Her naps have become restless, sweaty affairs, the pain now unceasing, surrounding her and fading, like the Doppler wail of an air-raid siren. She half imagines it will get better, like a fractured bone or the stomach flu, but of course it can only get worse. Worse than this!

She has Thanksgiving with Linda, Wayne, their family, and her daughters. They linger at the table for a long time, telling stories and drinking coffee, Cheri so exhausted by the effort of sitting upright that she mostly listens, watching their familiar faces in the warm light, attuned to the murmur of daughters in the kitchen, the comforting sound of water running. By the time she leaves—supported on either side by her girls, Linda following behind with leftovers to stow in the trunk—Cheri is so depleted that she can't keep the perilous thoughts at bay. She's nauseated with envy and rage, the unfairness of it all.

And of course, nobody truly understands, but she can't see how it would matter if they did. The sandbags, the diminished lung capacity, the clangorous pain. It's all so intensely personal and claustrophobic, the heightening present mixed up with the banal past—this morning she nearly swooned from the vertiginous sight of her old maple dresser rising and falling, a pistoning bedpost, and the striped-shirted body of her brother Sean flinging himself up and down as they jumped on her bed.

And last night she only catnapped, moving from bed to armchair and back to bed, dreaming random images of turkey farms, of rickrack on the neckline of a blouse, of the Beatles walking single file across a road. Once, right before dawn, she looked down in her dream and saw phosphorescent insects alight on her hands and arms.

I can't make it to Christmas, she tells them. I thought I could but I can't.

The news is devastating; she supposes it's possible none of them really believed it before now. The girls collapse against her and then grow strangely calm, wandering shell-shocked through the house, speaking to each other in thin echoing voices. Linda flinches when she's told, then breaks into tears, hands over her face.

They have three weeks to get used to it. After some consideration, Cheri chooses a Tuesday, the most nondescript day of the week. She calls Kevorkian's assistant, Neal, then books a flight to Detroit for December 16 and a night's lodging in a Bloomfield motel. According to the plan, that's where the suicide will occur. Her body will be taken from the motel to the hospital and then to the morgue, where somebody—the coroner?—will perform an autopsy.

She wants cremation, a small service, no flowers. Katy goes with her to make the arrangements and they try not to be too surreal about it but have to keep consulting their list.

The funeral director is a young man with intensely sincere eyes and pure, palpable compassion. Cheri grows sleepy in his presence, forgetting some of the things she meant to bring up.

"What about transporting my body if I should die elsewhere?" she asks.

"If you're choosing cremation," he says carefully, "then that can be done at a facility near where the death occurs." He pauses, thinks. "And we'll work directly with them to receive the, uh, from there." He stares at the backs of his hands for a moment, turning his wedding ring one way and then the other, an absentminded gesture that gives her time to fill in the blank.

Her body, reduced to a mound of kitty litter in a biscuit tin.

"Okay, then," she says, and they all stand, formally, and stare at one another. Katy is wearing the miserable look of someone waiting for a tetanus shot, determined to be brave for the nurse's sake. The funeral director touches Cheri's arm and looks into her eyes; his own are red-rimmed, which takes her by surprise.

People are so kind! She reels from it sometimes, the mute commiseration, the gestures of support and assistance so subtle she barely recognizes them as such. Katy, the first time she helped her mother take a bath, had seemed merely to be idling, recounting an anecdote, sitting on the closed toilet seat with her legs crossed, eyes roaming around the edges of the room. When Cheri had finished bathing, Katy lifted her out of the water—casually, still talking—and wrapped her in a towel. Never in the whole process (holding out the underwear to be stepped into, retrieving sweatpants warm from the dryer, tugging a pair of thick cotton socks onto the feet) did either of them let on that they'd performed a transposed version of this twenty years before.

Linda telephones people in their circle, urging them to visit now if they want the chance. A few friends stop by during the afternoons and evenings, bearing casserole dishes or loaves of bread. Putting the food away in the kitchen gives them time to compose themselves—they were warned, of course, but nevertheless it takes a moment. The deterioration has accelerated in the last days, ravaging her body but leaving her face as translucent and still as frosted glass. They kneel next to her rocking chair as they leave, keeping it together, promising to call in a few days, see how it's going.

Her breathing is labored after these visits, either from the exertion of talking and smiling or from suppressing the panic that rises up when she tells them goodbye, unable to confess her plan, to take proper leave of her friends. She retreats to her bedroom and lies on top of the covers, arms folded around a pillow to keep from coughing, tethered to an oxygen tank by a length of clear tubing. The cancer has taken over completely now, crowding her out of her own body. When she touches her chest, it's the monster she feels.

In eleven days it will be over. Eleven! Alone in her room, she whimpers with the terrible grief of it, of being forced to abandon herself like a smoldering ship. It's impossible to imagine not existing, she discovers, because in order to imagine, you must exist. The best she can do is picture the world as it is now, without her in it. But even then, she's the one picturing.

On the morning of day nine, she rests on the sofa and watches, absorbed, as a man climbs a telephone pole, his belt weighted with tools and an oversize red telephone receiver. He stabilizes himself with a safety harness and then gets busy untangling a skein of multicolored wires, holding the red handset to his ear, possibly even speaking into it, although she can't imagine to whom. Once, he takes pliers off his belt, gives something a good twist, and a sprig of snipped wire falls through the air to the grass below. Something about the scene, framed behind the glass of her living-room window, embodies what she's been struggling to understand. It's momentary, a flash of insight so brief it can't be seen but must be remembered, like the glimpse of a shooting star. The man with his cleats thrust into the pole, his weight tangible in the leather harness, the dark red of the telephone against the bright yellow of his hard hat, and then the tendril of wire falling away from his pliers—this is the world without her in it.

On the eighth day, she imagines dying with her eyes open, the naked vulnerability of it. She's got to remember to close her eyes and keep them closed, no matter what. And if Kevorkian approaches her and she panics or starts bawling, will he give her a chance to calm down or will he take it as a sign that she is conflicted, not ready, and refuse to go through with it? She forces herself to visualize the final scene over and over until it loses its meaning and becomes as ritualized as taking communion. No last-minute change of mind, no hysteria; she will simply greet him, explain herself in measured tones, express her gratitude, offer her arm for the needle, close her eyes.

By day seven, she understands air travel will be impossible, unendurable, because of her weakened state. A new plan is made for Wayne to rent a van and drive all of them to Detroit—Cheri, Linda, Sarah, and Kate. None of the others can be present at her actual death, of course, since it's illegal, but still, they'll be taking her there, nine hours away. Cheri feels momentarily frantic at the idea of this, her loved ones having to participate in her fate, but she can't hold on to it. Too sick, too busy grasping her own thin hand, pulling herself along. Almost overnight, she feels herself beginning to detach from them, not because she wants to, but because she needs her own full attention. This is simply part of what happens.

Linda comes over in the evening to wait

with them, a little blast of refreshing cold entering the house with her. She brings food as well and leans against the kitchen counter as they eat, chatting, then busies herself as best she can by sweeping up the fallen leaves from the schefflera tree, folding clean towels, petting Ursa. When she goes home, they resume the vigil, tiptoeing around the house in their sock feet, staring for long moments at the television or at their own spectral faces reflected in the dark windows.

Wayne shows up a few days before they are to leave and sits with Cheri awhile, making quiet small talk until she tires and then saying goodbye, squeezing her hand momentarily before he stands. Sarah and Katy call to him from the backyard, where Ursa has chased one of the cats up a tree. They are near tears, both of them walking in circles, trying to coax the cat down in high urgent voices. Wayne climbs a few feet up the tree and lifts the cat off a branch, manually detaching each claw, hands it down to Sarah. When he glances back,

Cheri is standing at the kitchen window, waving thank you.

On the last night, Linda makes sandwiches for the trip, egg salad with lettuce, while Wayne plots the route using a road map and his computer; Sarah and Katy, after a dinner of yogurt and leftover soup, place the cats in bed with their mother and watch as she pets them and they purr, as Ursa puts her nose up on the covers and gets her ears combed and her face kissed; they listen as she reminds them: I love you, my *chicas*, never forget.

And Cheri, on her last night, weeps with relief when she's finally alone, suffers about five minutes of teeth-chattering fear, calms herself by imagining the faces and whispering the names of all her past dogs, then lies quietly with the pillow pressed to her chest, watching the interior images that click on and off like slides.

Near dawn, she sleeps for a while and dreams of gathering Easter eggs: a violet one nestled between the white pickets of a porch railing, a pink-and-green one camouflaged in the grass next to a wire fence, an azure one balanced perfectly and precariously on a water spigot.

They leave under cover of darkness, like duck hunters or criminals, barely whispering. They settle Cheri on the bench seat in the middle of the van, oxygen canister next to her, daughters behind her. The van door glides closed with a soft thud, and while Wayne climbs in and situates his coffee, Linda stares out the windows at the neighborhood emerging in the grainy light. Straight-edged prairie bungalows surrounded by sugar maples and oaks, Cheri's little corner house painted a curious shade of dark vanilla with bright white trim; a thatch of low evergreens pressed against the porch. It all seems so calm and unadorned, as full of hidden promise as the bulbs planted beneath the kitchen window.

Cheri refuses herself even one last look. That was then; this is now.

She needs more oxygen already, just from the effort of getting this far. Linda turns on the dome light and adjusts the dial; Cheri breathes deeply, head down to combat the nausea. Sarah begins crying silently in the back, and Katy leans forward to touch her mother's shoulder. The town flattens into countryside and they drive due east, straight into the sunrise, pillowy December clouds edged in apricot. Linda passes the thermos to Katy, and Cheri lifts her head briefly, asks to have the oxygen turned up again.

Halfway through Illinois, she begins to panic over possibly having to go to the hospital if the tank runs out and can't be refilled. She had made all the plans for the trip, including how much oxygen to bring, but her needs have increased sharply over just the last few days. If she has to go to the hospital, they'll call her doctor, and her doctor will put two and two together. Inside the tight black place behind her eyelids, she watches herself clench her fists and hold them up against the sky.

Wayne tracks down a pharmacy in Joliet, and Linda somehow gets the tank refilled.

All they know is she walked in with it empty and walked out with it full. Determination and twenty-five bucks, she tells them. Cheri keeps her head in her hands through the next two states, trying not to vomit. Sarah and Kate take turns comforting her and resting their foreheads on the back of her seat, dazed and leaden. Car crazy, longing for a cigarette.

Cheri lifts her head briefly and seeks out Wayne in the rearview mirror. "I need to stop at a bathroom," she tells him.

He finds a funky, old-fashioned Clark station where he can pull right up to the washroom door. Two of them help her use the facilities while the other two lean against the van and smoke. Cheri has never been this freaked out in her life, and that's saying something. One thing she's learning is that it's important to stay in the moment, not to leap ahead even fifteen minutes. Right now, she's staring at herself in a shadowed washroom mirror; now she's in the cold wind next to the car trying to get her gloves on. Now they slide the door open and she steps back, looks at her daughter's face. Now she's getting settled, taking the oxygen tube, returning the stare of the guy pumping gas. Frozen cornfields, a deflated barn, a looming underpass, and then the interstate. She drops her head down into the cool damp shell of her hands. Now the buffet and roar of semis, now a quavering sigh from somebody inside the van. The tires begin making a rhythmic clicking noise, passing over seams in the concrete.

Cheri opens her eyes intermittently and stares at her knees, just to stabilize and remember where she is. Lying down isn't possible, although that's why they got the van. Her lungs are full, and the nausea is overwhelming. Breathless and gasping, she runs down a twisting white corridor inside her head, the blat of a siren bouncing off the walls; suddenly the narrow hallway opens out onto a suburban backyard, the floor becomes grass, and she's on a swing, knobby knees pumping, reaching toward the sky with her Keds. The chains go slack for a long instant each time the swing reaches its apex. She's panting with reckless exhilaration.

"Do you need it turned up?" Linda's voice, disembodied, and the monster inches away; Cheri's breathing calms.

"Thank you," she whispers into her hands.

The swing now has stopped, and, still seated, she walks herself around in a circle, twisting the chains, then lifts her feet and spins, body canted so far back that her hair brushes the dirt. She's breathless and dizzy under the limp August sky until someone reaches out, turns up a radio, and cold invigorating oxygen flows into her nose. Another someone gently stabilizes her as the van banks onto an exit, takes a left turn, glides over a bump, ascends, descends, and stops. When she looks up from her cupped hands, they are idling under the canopy of a Quality Inn.

*Thank God.* She retreats into her hands again.

Behind the registration desk is a holiday wreath and a mirror; in the mirror is the face of a crazy person who looks only marginally like Sarah. She pulls it together as best she can—tucking in the migrating strands of hair, straightening her jacket, clearing her throat—before meeting the eyes of the clerk. He's a man in his fifties, white-haired, wearing glasses.

"My mother reserved a room," she tells him. "Cheri Tremble?"

He stares at her, assessing. "Where is she?" he asks.

"I'm getting the room," Sarah answers slowly. "She's in the car, with a headache."

He continues staring at her for a moment, then steps into an office and calls someone, speaking low but keeping an eye on the desk and the young woman shifting from foot to foot, zipping and unzipping her coat.

Sarah deliberately turns her back on him. The lobby is awash in a franchised gloom—couches here and there, glass coffee table with an extravagant arrangement of silk flowers, and a breakfast station with a do-it-yourself waffle iron and plastic bins that dispense cornflakes. The clerk steps up once again to the desk; the wreath behind his head is decorated with spray-on snow and sparkling plastic fruit made to look like marzipan. He knows what's going on.

"I'm sorry, I can't give you a room," he tells her.

"Why not?" she asks, incredulous.

"We've had some problems with Dr. Kevorkian," he says. He looks pleased, which frightens Sarah. She thought he was calling his boss, but it could have been the police. He has the excited and pious expression of a man capable of making a citizen's arrest.

"This is crazy," she answers, backing away. "We have a reservation."

"Huh-uh," he says loudly. "Nope."

And then Sarah's back in the van, telling Wayne to drive, get out of there; Cheri's struggling to breathe, unable to make a decision, all of them thrown into a panic that propels them out of the parking lot and back into the early-evening traffic. They drive around in circles for a few minutes until they find a pay phone and Linda leaves a message for Kevorkian's assistant, Neal Nicol. They wait as long as they can, motor idling in the cold, rainy twilight, oxygen tank dwindling, Cheri suffering wave after wave of anxiety. The fear of dying tonight is nothing, she realizes, compared to the fear of still being alive tomorrow morning. She leans forward and then back, rocking herself slowly, trying to calm down. No one returns the call, and after a while they pull away reluctantly and drive a few blocks more to an Office Depot.

Linda, Katy, and Sarah go inside and compose a fax to Kevorkian, explaining their predicament in all caps:

TO: DOCTOR
FROM: CHERI'S FRIEND

CHERI TREMBLE IS IN THE DETROIT AREA. SHE WAS NOT PERMITTED TO REGISTER AT THE QUALITY INN ... WE HAVE TRIED TO REACH NEAL A NUMBER OF TIMES WITHOUT SUCCESS AND WE ONLY HAVE ONE SMALL TANK OF O2 LEFT ... WE ARE FAXING THIS FROM OFFICE DEPOT IN BLOOMFIELD.

The store is warm and well lit; a man stands in line near them holding a wastebasket and a package of Bic pens. The boy at the copy counter takes their fax and sends it without comment, then lingers nearby, casting sidelong glances at Katy. A few feet away, down the office-equipment aisle, a young couple in matching ski jackets feed a piece of paper into a shredder and watch as it emerges in long, graceful strands.

The phone rings and a fax begins chugging through.

*Thank God*, Linda whispers.

Sarah and Kate stand next to the car in twilight, smoking and waiting for Neal, who is on his way. The drizzle stops momentarily and one by one, the parking-lot floodlights buzz to life, turning everything green. Inside the van, just visible through the smoky glass, Cheri is sitting once again with head in hands.

"This is fun," Katy says.

"Yeah," Sarah answers.

They can hardly look at each other,

faces bathed in the alien light. Each knows what the other is feeling, being so urgently compelled toward something they are profoundly and instinctively opposed to. Not Kevorkian, exactly, but the simple fact of Cheri's death. Neither of them has fully absorbed the fact that if all goes as planned, she will cease to exist *this evening*. This evening! They scan the faces in the cars that glide past, easing into and out of parking spaces, people on their way to buy envelopes. Before anyone has a chance to get worried, a car pulls up, and a large man jumps out and hugs them. Neal. They're to follow him to Kevorkian's house.

They wind through an affluent neighborhood, past suburban castles with iron gates and leafless, glowering trees; inside the van the only sound in the long interval between the windshield wipers is the wheeze of oxygen moving through the tubing. It's trash day in this neighborhood, garbage cans materializing and dematerializing in the thin steam that rises from the streets. They follow Neal up the driveway of an unassuming ranch house tucked among the sprawling mansions. Suddenly, a man is framed in their headlights, peeking out from the at- tached garage. Gaunt and sunken-eyed, with a military crew cut and an animated expression, he gestures for them to pull in- side and then hops nimbly out of their way.

Jack Kevorkian, as seen on TV.

Relieved and terrified, everyone bursts out laughing, even Cheri.

The burden is shifted, somehow, with that momentary release of hysteria. In his cardigan sweater and open-collared shirt, Kevorkian has the amiable and authoritar- ian air of a retired general. He is clearly the center of the group, in control, his voice resonant and welcoming as he introduces himself and Dr. Georges Reding—a psychi- atrist who, along with Neal, will remain in the background as witness and assistant.

Wayne half carries Cheri into the living room, where plastic chairs have been ar- ranged in a semicircle, one of them draped with a blanket to make it more comfort- able. Katy sits next to her mother; Sarah sits at their feet. Whatever numbness had gotten them all through the long ride from Iowa is wearing off. The house feels temporary, like an office set up in a trailer, and the men seem both hearty and furtive, like Bible salesmen.

Cheri is awake now, unintimidated. These men are familiar to her; she understands the dynamics of idealism, the personality traits of a certain kind of fanaticism. She rallies, gives a coherent account of her medical condition. They want to ascertain that this is her decision.

"Yes, mine," she says clearly. She holds her oxygen tube out like the stem of a wineglass and gathers herself before speaking again. "I have only forty-five minutes of oxygen left."

"We have time," Dr. Kevorkian says kindly. "Don't worry."

Katy and Sarah stare at each other, wide-eyed and trembling. Forty-five minutes is fifteen times three. Everything is welling up, faster than they can absorb it.

Dr. Kevorkian speaks to all of them,

describing what he calls a patholytic procedure, the intravenous injection of a combination of drugs that will make her go to sleep, relax her respirations, and stop her heart. Cheri listens carefully, nodding, and then signs her name over and over, *Cheri Tremble*, until she's hearing it inside her head like a chant.

Linda and Wayne must sign papers as well, and they are told to leave the state via the most direct route possible. It's all printed out for them: the coroner, the funeral home, what to do and when.

Cheri hands her driver's license to Kevorkian for identification of the body, then gives her billfold, address book, and glasses to Sarah.

It's time.

And now the girls are dissolving, wailing, saying their goodbyes in a chaos of hands, mouths, faces, hair, tears. At one point or another, both are in Cheri's lap, holding on to her, crying so violently and so desperately that everyone is trying to shush them. They're inconsolable; every time they pull themselves away and start toward the door, they turn back to their mother. Cheri is trying to soothe them, kissing foreheads, whispering. Her tank now says thirty-two minutes.

She says a hurried goodbye to Linda and Wayne, reaching up to embrace them weakly, then watching as they gather her daughters and try to lead them from the house, each one breaking away briefly, running back to kneel at Cheri's feet, sobbing.

Cheri calls out to Linda, "Take care of them!"

"I will," Linda promises, her face haggard and despairing. It's all a jagged blur of grief: the careening house, Katy's heaving shoulders and Sarah's stricken face, Wayne's jacket-clad arm as he tries to usher them from the room, Linda's own unspoken words of farewell fluttering inside her chest like snared birds.

At the door, Sarah turns and starts back toward her mother again. *You can't just leave a person like this,* she thinks. *You can't.*

"Sarah!" Cheri says sharply.

Sarah stops. Her mother is sitting in the draped chair, the three men standing in the shadows behind her. *You can't leave a person like this.* But she sees from her mother's expression that it's too late.

Cheri is leaving them.

*

When they're gone, the house is filled with a beautiful, queer silence. It's like the airy, suspended moment that follows the last reverberating note on a pipe organ. *I'm alone,* she thinks, her heart suddenly clopping inside her chest like hooves, her head too heavy for the fragile stem of her neck. No family, no friends, no way out except through. She slumps forward in a swoon and then immediately rights herself, overcompensating like a drunk. *Please,* she thinks, picturing herself erect and composed. *I'm sorry.*

When the men first touch her, she flinches and cries out but then grows calm as they minister to her. Two of them help her down the hall to a small bedroom, prop her up with pillows to ease her breathing, tuck a rolled-up blanket under her knees, cover her with a thin blue chenille bedspread.

Dr. Kevorkian takes a seat next to her. He explains that the tank is at eighteen minutes, and when it's at ten, if she's ready, he will start the procedure. Cheri half closes her eyes and reaches out, entwines her fingers with this stranger's. She's beyond words now, transfixed by the images flickering inside her head, left hand gripping the folds of chenille.

At first it's meaningless, frantic electrical impulses taking the form of memories—a Mexican lizard on an adobe wall, panting like a dog; a pair of dusty ankles; her father in a sports coat, nuzzling a kitten; her brother Sean with a sparkler framed against a night sky, spelling out her name with big cursive flourishes, the letters disappearing even as they are written. And then the pain is gone, leached out of her so completely that she feels hollow and weightless, borne aloft, the back of her head tucked into the crook of someone's elbow, legs bent as they were in the womb, flannel feet cupped in the palm of a hand. Spellbound, she uses her last minutes to gaze up at her mother's young face.

Cheri?

She nods, still watching her mother, and someone takes her arm.

The needle is cold, and in a moment she's numb, separated from the men by a thick layer of ice. She breathes slowly in the narrow pocket of air, and the children in their bright skates congregate above her head. She lingers there for a moment, her cheek pressed against the underside of the ice, until a hand reaches down and pushes her under.

# Author's Note

In December 1997, Cheri Tremble committed suicide with the assistance of Dr Jack Kevorkian. What you have just read is a merging of fact with fiction: The external details of Cheri's life and illness are as accurate as possible, gleaned from interviews with her friends and family, while the internal details – her thoughts, her memories, and what occurred after her loved ones saw her for the last time – are imagined.